THE STORY
of
RAINBOW
BEAR

JESSICA PERRI

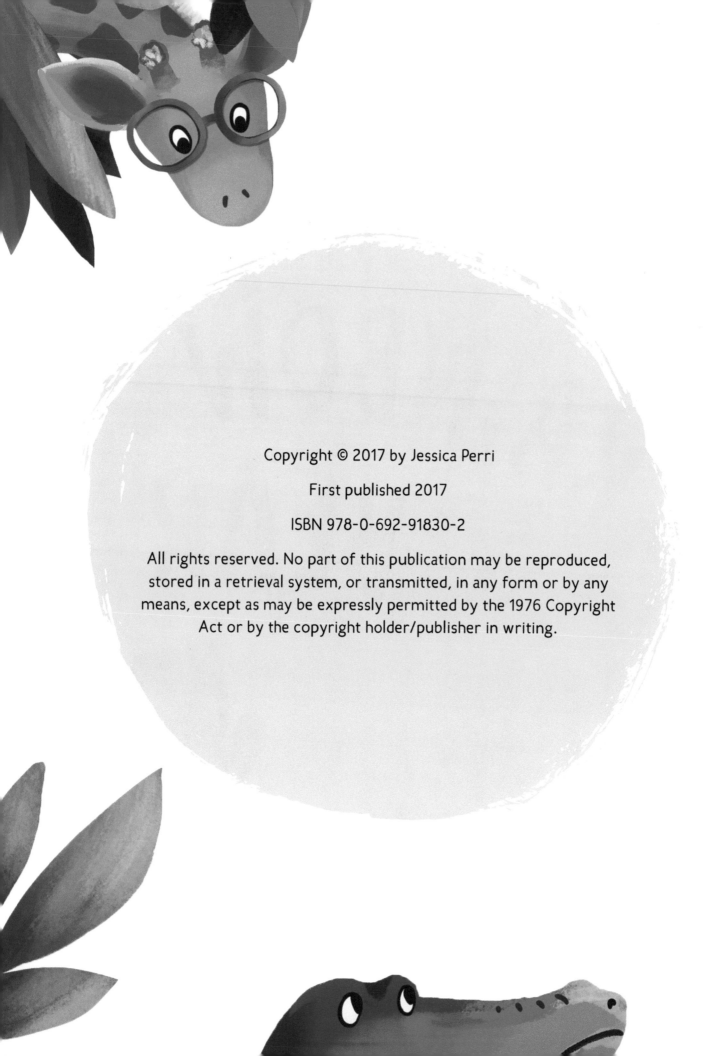

Across the river and deep in the woods, there is a place called *Bear Forest* where all kinds of bears live. Small bears, big bears, round bears, tall bears.

On a dark, rainy day in Bear Forest, a bear cub was born. Mama
Bear looked up at the stormy sky and watched raindrops pour
down on her little cub. She named him Rain Bear.

Rain Bear quickly grew. He loved growing up in Bear Forest with all his bear family and friends.

The bears loved to do everything together like riding bikes,
playing games, and swimming in the lake.

When Rain Bear turned five, it was time to go to school in the big city. Mama Bear told him that he would make new friends from all over.

But Rain Bear did not want to go. He wanted to stay in Bear Forest with his bear family and friends.

Rain Bear walked into his first day of school and looked around the classroom. There were crocodiles, tigers, birds, and elephants, but no other bear in sight.

He watched as all the other animals met each other, smiling and laughing. But Rain Bear sat in the corner thinking, "These animals are not like me. We will never be friends."

As the days went by, Rain Bear kept to himself.

He felt sad and lonely, and a rain cloud appeared in the sky.

But then, one day during recess, a red monkey came over and said, "Do you like to ride bikes?" Rain Bear loved biking! He grabbed a bike and pedaled.

As the two rode around the playground, Rain Bear saw that they were not so different after all. He smiled, and bright, red stripes appeared on his fur.

Rain Bear walked into the library to see a tall, orange giraffe reading a book. The giraffe waved at Rain Bear. "Come read with me," he said.

As they read together, Rain Bear smiled, and bright, orange stripes appeared on his fur.

After school, Rain Bear saw a bright kite in the sky. He looked down and saw a little, yellow bird who said, "Hi! Do you want to fly kites with me?"

As the two watched the pretty kites fly in the sky, Rain Bear was glad to make another friend. He smiled, and bright, yellow stripes appeared on his fur.

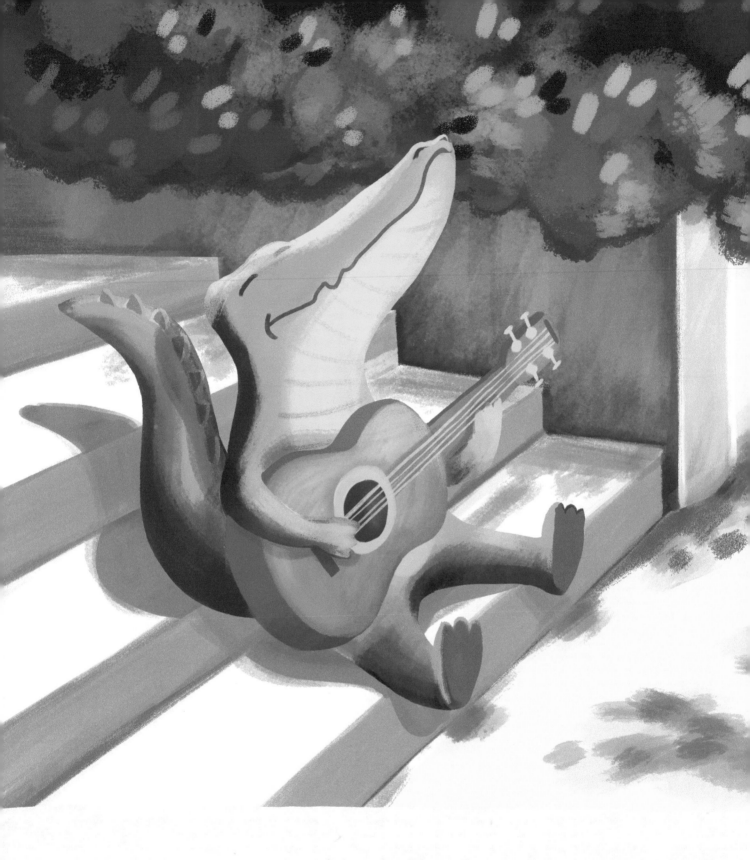

Walking to the bus, Rain Bear heard a beautiful noise behind him. He turned around to see a green crocodile strumming a guitar. "Hi, Rain Bear! Do you play any instruments?"

Rain Bear pulled out a harmonica from his backpack and joined in. He smiled, and bright, green stripes appeared on his fur.

Rain Bear went to the lake and saw a blue elephant swimming in the water. The elephant said, "The water is nice! Jump in!"

As they splashed around in the cool water, Rain Bear smiled, and bright, blue stripes appeared on his fur.

A purple bunny joined the school. During recess, Rain Bear
saw the bunny sitting on a swing by himself. Rain Bear said
"Hi, Purple Bunny! Come play with us!"

The bunny hopped over, and Rain Bear saw the bunny smile.
He smiled back. And bright, purple stripes appeared on his fur.

Rain Bear was so happy that he made so many good friends.
Each friend was special in their own way, but they also had
many things in common.

Rain Bear looked down at his fur. It had become a rainbow of colors. All of his friends looked at him and said, "You don't look like a Rain Bear...you look like a Rainbow Bear!" And from that day on, that is what they called him. Rainbow Bear.

CPSIA information can be obtained
at www.ICGtesting.com
Printed in the USA
BVHW022309211221
624593BV00007BA/695